Vic   APR 2 1 2009

ATOS Book Level: ___3.3___
AR Points: ___0.5___
Quiz #: _108502_ [X] RP [ ] LS [ ] VP
Lexile: ___430___

DAMIAN DROOTH SUPERSLEUTH

THE CASE OF THE DISAPPEARING DAUGHTER

by Barbara Mitchelhill

illustrated by Tony Ross

Librarian Reviewer
Marci Peschke
Librarian, Dallas Independent School District
MA Education Reading Specialist, Stephen F. Austin State University
Learning Resources Endorsement, Texas Women's University

Reading Consultant
Elizabeth Stedem
Educator/Consultant, Colorado Springs, CO
MA in Elementary Education, University of Denver, CO

STONE ARCH BOOKS
Minneapolis   San Diego

First published in the United States in 2007
by Stone Arch Books,
151 Good Counsel Drive, P.O. Box 669,
Mankato, Minnesota 56002.
www.stonearchbooks.com

First published in 2000
by Andersen Press Ltd, London.

Library of Congress Cataloging-in-Publication Data
Mitchelhill, Barbara.
    The Case of the Disappearing Daughter / by Barbara Mitchelhill;
illustrated by Tony Ross.
    p. cm. — (Pathway Books) (Damian Drooth Supersleuth)
    Summary: Young Damian Drooth puts his newly-acquired detective
skills to the test when the daughter of a wealthy movie director is kidnapped
from the set.
    ISBN-13: 978-1-59889-119-5 (hardcover)
    ISBN-10: 1-59889-119-7 (hardcover)
    ISBN-13: 978-1-59889-269-7 (paperback)
    ISBN-10: 1-59889-269-X (paperback)
    [1. Kidnapping—Fiction. 2. Motion pictures—Production and
direction—Fiction. 3. Mystery and detective stories.] I. Ross, Tony, ill.
II. Title. III. Series. IV. Series: Mitchelhill, Barbara. Damian Drooth
Supersleuth.
PZ7.M697Casd 2007
[Fic]—dc22   2006007179

Art Director: Heather Kindseth
Graphic Designer: Kay Fraser

1 2 3 4 5 6 11 10 09 08 07 06

Printed in the United States of America.

Table of Contents

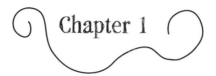

Chapter 1

My name is Drooth. Damian Drooth. I track down criminals and solve crimes. A kind of one-kid, clean-up-the-world service.

How did I start?

It was last year. Summer vacation had started and I was bored! You know how it is when all your friends are away at the beach or, even worse, at Disneyland.

I was riding on a bus and feeling
miserable when I noticed a book on
the seat next to me. "A Hundred Ways
to Catch a Criminal." I had nothing
better to do, so I read it.

After that I was hooked! My
life changed overnight. I was a
supersleuth, and my mission was to rid
the world of crime.

As it turned out, I didn't have long to wait.

I was in the supermarket that afternoon. I was heading for the frozen pizza section when I saw a man behind the freezers. That is so suspicious! I thought. That man is a villain! If I was going to stop a crime, I had to act fast. So I climbed up on a shelf and shouted, "Thief! Over there! Get him!"

For a second, everybody in the supermarket stood still and stared at me. Then they rushed over to the frozen foods section. The crook was shaking with fear.

Shoppers surrounded him. Some people bashed him with their shopping baskets. He was finished, I could tell.

Me? I stayed cool and walked out.

That was my first day as a crime buster. Pretty good, huh? But there was more. On the way home, I saw a man snatch a woman's purse. He threw it into a big black SUV and drove off.

A getaway car! I knew about them.

I pulled out my detective notebook and scribbled down the license plate number.

Then I dashed down the street to find a telephone.

But Mom didn't see things the same way I did.

On Friday, she got two letters.

Dear Madam,

Please keep your son out of our supermarket. My store detective does not like being accused of shoplifting by a small boy. He was very upset.
He was only doing his job.

Yours sincerely,

PJ Handy

Manager, Save-a-lot Superstore

Dear Mrs. Drooth,

No thanks to your son, I almost spent last night in jail.
Please explain to him that I was putting an old lady's shopping bag into my taxi. I was not stealing it.

A. L. Fair

Ace Taxi Company

When Mom read the letters, her face
turned a weird shade of purple. This
happens when she gets angry. I think
she should go see a doctor.

Chapter 2

I have to admit, I made mistakes at first. So I started studying seriously. I wanted to be the best private eye ever. I watched tons of movies. I sat in my pajamas in the living room with the curtains closed all day long.

Mom wasn't impressed. "It's sunny outside," she said. "Why don't you play games like the other kids? It's not natural."

It's difficult to be a supersleuth in my neighborhood, but I was determined!

By the end of the week I had watched so many crimes being solved in movies that I worked out my very first detective theory.

This is my theory:

People whose eyes are very close together are not to be trusted and are up to no good. They are probably criminals.

With this theory, I knew I was ready to start my career.

I would go out and track down crooks, swindlers, bank robbers, and forgers.

It was going to be a lot of work. I decided to start the next day.

The next day, Mom saw me slipping out of the back door in my detective outfit. She looked at me suspiciously.

"Just going to solve a crime, Mom," I explained.

She slammed the door shut. "No way, Damian," she said. "I want to keep my eye on you. You can forget this detective stuff. I don't want any more embarrassing letters."

That was bad news. Did James Bond ever have problems like that? Was Sherlock Holmes ever kept in the house by his mom? No! I was upset.

"You can come to work with me," said Mom. "That will keep you out of trouble."

Mom runs a company called Home Cooking Unlimited. She cooks for weddings and parties and stuff like that.

When she takes me with her, I always get stuck washing the dishes. I hate that. It's so boring.

"I'm working at Harbury Hall today," she said as we packed the van with a million bread rolls. "There's a film crew working up there all week."

A film crew? Actors. Camera operators. Stunt artists. I started to be more excited.

"Don't get any funny ideas," said Mom. "You're doing the dishes."

I knew it.

Once we were at Harbury Hall, Mom carried piles of plates into the food tent.

(I am not allowed to carry things because of a little accident I had last year. Can I help it if plates are slippery?)

I sat and ate my early morning bag of chips and read the newspaper. We detectives have to keep up to date.

It was full of stories of unsolved crimes. The police clearly needed help. And there I was trapped in a food tent.

What a waste of a brilliant mind!

Things brightened up later. A man called Victor DeVito came into the tent. As it turned out, Mr. DeVito was the movie director.

A real big shot!

He didn't go anywhere without a crowd of people. I had never met a movie director before.

But I stayed cool. I kept my little autograph book in my pocket. I'd wait until later.

"Howdy, ma'am!" he said to my Mom. "I just stopped by to introduce myself. You catering folk are real important on the set. Yes, sir!"

I could tell Mom was pleased. She smiled and her cheeks turned pink.

"And who are you, sonny?" he said to me.

"Damian Drooth, Supersleuth," I said.

Then I showed him the business card I'd made the night before.

He was very impressed.

"Well, Damian! There are plenty of crooks in the movie business. Watch out for them, will you?" he asked.

My first job! I was going to be a crime watcher on a film set. Wow! I couldn't promise to catch every crook, but I'd do my best.

I was on the lookout.

Chapter 3

Mr. DeVito had a daughter named Trixibelle. You could tell Trixibelle's dad was rich. She had everything. Cool shoes. A fur coat. An MP3 player. She stayed behind when her dad went to check out cameras and stuff. She gave me a pack of Charley Chip's Chocolate Drops. She had tons.

"You're so lucky, Damian," she said as we sat eating. "You've got a mom who cooks for you. My mom's just an actress, you know. She's never home. Right now she's in Hong Kong."

"Acting's really interesting," I said.

Trixibelle shook her head. "It's not as interesting as cooking. That's what I want to do when I grow up. But Pops says I'll be too rich to be a cook."

Being rich sounded pretty good to me. At least you didn't get stuck doing the dishes.

Somebody called Trixibelle's name outside the tent.

"That's my new tutor, Miss Berry," Trixibelle said. She sighed. "I have to go."

I was amazed. I'd never met anyone with a personal tutor. But then I'd never met anyone as rich as the DeVito family.

Trixibelle walked away from the tent. Her tutor was waiting by the large white trailer across from the tent.

Wow! I thought. Is that lady really Trixibelle's teacher?

She looked like a movie star! She was tall with long blonde hair and red lipstick. And she was wearing really cool sunglasses, too.

She was nothing like Mr. Grimethorpe, our class teacher.

Lucky Trixibelle!

By 10:30, there was a long line outside the food tent.

Hungry actors. Starving technicians.

They all wanted Mom's coffee and cake. Soon, I was up to my elbows in dirty dishwater.

After an hour and a half of washing dishes, my hands had turned ghostly white. They were as wrinkled as prunes.

"If you can't do it faster than that, Damian, we'll never be ready for lunch," Mom said with a moan.

I admit I wasn't the fastest dishwasher in the world.

It was hard keeping my mind on dirty plates.

Luckily, I was saved from total boredom when one of the security guards stuck his head into the tent.

"Anybody seen Trixibelle?" he asked.

I lifted my hands out of the water. "She's in the trailer over there," I said, pointing across the grass.

The guard shook his head. "Not for half an hour," he said.

"Her tutor reported her missing," he added. "Miss Berry went out to get a cup of coffee and when she got back, Trixibelle was gone."

"I'll find her," I said. "I'm great at tracking down missing people."

This was not exactly true.

But it was a good excuse to get away from the dishes.

Mom didn't look happy when the guard told her. Her lips were pressed tight together.

"Damian's got work to do," she said.

The guard's eyes looked serious.

"Mr. DeVito will be very angry if we lose his daughter," he said in a threatening kind of way. "Your son would be a great help."

So Mom let me go.

That was how the Case of the Disappearing Daughter began.

Chapter 4

I wasn't really that worried about Trixibelle. I just figured she had gone off somewhere to get away from her homework.

I knew all about that. I had done the same thing myself.

I followed the guard across the grass.

Miss Berry was standing by the trailer.

She was upset.

She had a large tissue held to her
nose and she was sniffing.

"Try not to worry, Miss Berry," I said.
"I'll get her back for you. You can
count on me."

She gave me a wonderful smile and
a tingle ran from the top of my head
down to my toes. I felt like a brave
knight in shining armor.

Everyone was out searching for Trixibelle, except Mom, who was doing the dishes.

The whole crew had stopped work to look for her. I used all my detective skills but I couldn't find anything. Not a single clue.

Suddenly, Victor DeVito came rushing out of his trailer and climbed onto its roof. Was the man crazy, or what? I wondered.

"Listen, people!" he shouted through his megaphone.

Everything went deathly quiet.

"I have some terrible news. My
Trixibelle has been kidnapped!"

There were gasps of oohs and aaahs.
Nobody could believe it.

"It's true!" the director continued, holding his hand up for silence. (Mr. Grimethorpe, our class teacher, often does this.)

"I just got a phone call and some crazy people are demanding a million dollars for my baby."

He took a large handkerchief and blew his nose.

"I'll pay it if I have to, but in the meantime, the police are doing their best to find out where she is."

I know for a fact that the police often miss clues that are right under their noses. So I decided that I would have to track down the criminals. After all, Victor DeVito himself had asked me to be on the lookout for crooks. It was the least I could do.

Chapter 5

I hurried back to tell Mom about the kidnapping.

"I heard," she said. "Miss Berry is very upset. She's gone to lie down."

Poor Miss Berry! I thought. She must be feeling really guilty since she let Mr. DeVito's daughter slip away.

"I think I'll take her a cup of tea," I said. "She'll like that." It would be a good chance to impress Miss Berry with my detective ideas for finding Trixibelle.

"That's thoughtful of you, Damian,"
said Mom. I could tell she was surprised.

I was careful not to spill the tea as I
pushed open the trailer door. I suppose
I should have knocked — but I didn't.
What I saw shocked me.

Miss Berry wasn't lying down at all.

She was stuffing piles of clothes into a big suitcase.

I scanned the trailer with my detective laser vision. On a table were a pair of shades and a long blonde wig. I gasped. Then Miss Berry stood up and turned around. What a shock! She wasn't blonde after all. She had short dark hair.

"Oh dear!" she said, grabbing her wig. "I'm such a mess, Damian! I was just keeping myself busy. Just cleaning up." She slammed the suitcase shut and took the cup of tea.

"How very kind of you, dear boy. Poor, poor Trixibelle," she said. She smiled, but she couldn't fool me. Things had changed.

I could see that her eyes were set very close together. If my theory was right, Miss Berry was a criminal in disguise.

Chapter 6

After that, I decided to keep an eye on the trailer. This was hard, because Mom made me finish washing the dishes. I had to keep looking over my shoulder. My neck hurt. It was awful.

Nothing happened for a while. Then Mom asked me to take the garbage out.

Just as I left the tent, I saw Miss Berry sneaking out of the trailer. She was carrying a suitcase!

I dumped the garbage bag and followed her, keeping my distance, just like detectives do.

Before long, I realized that she was heading for the parking lot. If she had a car, she could be fifty miles away in no time! Then my main suspect would be lost forever.

She stopped by a large red car and took some keys from her handbag.

I dropped down between two vans and watched. My heart was pounding like a rock band. She was going to escape. How could I stop her?

As she opened the car door, a voice shouted, "Hey you! Wait!"

Miss Berry spun around. A security guard was hurrying toward her.

"You're not leaving, are you?" the guard asked.

Miss Berry's piggy eyes nearly popped out of her head.

I could see that she was shaking. "Just going for a little ride," she said, trying to sound calm.

"Mr. DeVito said nobody should leave," said the guard firmly. He was pretty scary.

But Miss Berry smiled and walked around the car. "I'm so upset, officer. Trixibelle is my pupil, you see."

I could tell that the guard thought she was a movie star. She stood there telling him lies, and he believed her!

It was clear he wasn't trained well in detective work.

I didn't waste any time. While they were talking on one side of the car, I crept around the other side. Slowly, I opened the back door. I slipped in and lay down on the floor behind the driver's seat. Wherever Miss Berry went, I'd go too!

Chapter 7

Miss Berry drove like a maniac. She whizzed around turns. She zoomed down hills. I felt sick. When I heard the beeps that meant she was dialing her cell phone, I couldn't believe it!

She couldn't drive with two hands, and it was even worse when she just used one!

"Zac! It's me," she said. "I'm on my way. Are you ready to move the girl? DeVito should come up with the money within the next hour."

So my theory about close-set eyes was right. Miss Berry was a criminal. A kidnapper! But I was on her trail.

All I had to do was get Trixibelle out of her clutches.

When she finally screeched to a halt, my head smashed against the back of the driver's seat.

My brain was spinning. I heard the
car door open and close, and then Miss
Berry walked away. Somehow, I had to
get up!

I was seeing stars, but I pulled myself
together. I peeked out the window.

We were in a deserted farmyard.

There was no sign of Miss Berry. Just lots of barns and old sheds.

It was a perfect hiding place. Nobody would come to a place like that. The problem was that I didn't know where to start looking. Trixibelle could be anywhere.

I opened the car door and slid onto the ground. Like a marine on a combat mission, I crawled across the farmyard.

Except for the noise of birds twittering, there wasn't a sound. No voices. Nothing.

I stood up. I pressed my back to the fence and hoped Miss Berry wasn't looking out of one of the windows.

My forehead was sticky with sweat.

I raced across to a large barn.
I stopped by a doorway and stood
there, panting.

That was when my luck changed.
I glanced down and saw a trail of
chocolate drops.

They were Charley Chip's Chocolate
Drops. I could spot them from a mile
away. Trixibelle had left a clue! I
felt hopeful.

I walked through the door of the
barn and climbed some stone steps.

It was dark inside and I had to use
my hands to feel my way. Luckily, the
chocolate drops led right to a wooden
door at the top. I pressed my ear
against it.

Voices! That guy named Zac and Miss Berry!

I panicked. I needed help. I had to run. I had to get away!

I was about to turn around and go back when the worst thing possible happened. The door opened.

"You!" said Miss Berry.

"Who's he?" yelled the man. (He must have been Zac.)

Miss Berry leaned forward to grab me.

I stepped backward.

Miss Berry slipped.

Zac tripped over her.

Smash! They crashed down the stairs.

Bang! Clunk! Boing!

At the bottom, they even knocked some bales of hay on top of them. There they lay, moaning. Only their feet and arms could be seen. What a sight!

Trixibelle was in a room upstairs, tied to a chair. No problem! I had her free in a flash.

"You're wonderful, Damian," she said. She flung her arms around my neck and gave me a sloppy kiss.

I was so embarrassed. "Don't mention it," I said. "It was nothing."

We raced downstairs where the two kidnappers were lying moaning under the bales. Their arms were flapping about but they couldn't move.

"Sit on them," I said. "That way they can't get away."

Trixi sat on her tutor. I sat on Zac.

The question was, what should we do next? If one of us went for help, one of the kidnappers could get free.

We couldn't stay here forever. My brain was pounding, trying to find a solution to our problem.

What would Sherlock Holmes do? What would Superman do?

"We could always use my cell phone," said Trixibelle.

She fished a phone out of her pocket and dialed 911. She was smarter than I thought.

Chapter 8

In no time, the barn was surrounded. Five police cars showed up, along with SUVs bringing Victor DeVito and the entire film crew.

"We're here, babe!" shouted Mr. DeVito through his megaphone. "Your daddy's here to get you."

Miss Berry and Zac were soon locked up in a police car.

We went back to Harbury Hall and Victor DeVito threw a fantastic party.

There were mountains of food and I didn't have to wash any dishes.

"I'm proud of you, Damian," said Trixi's dad.

My mom nodded and wiped a tear from her eye."

It was all a little embarrassing. "It's the training," I explained. "I'm a famous supersleuth in my hometown. It was all in a day's work."

Victor nodded as if he understood. I could tell he was very impressed.

Afterwards the police inspector came to talk to me. I think he wanted to pick up some tips on solving crimes.

"A real detective looks for clues," I said. "That's what I did."

He pulled his notebook out, ready to jot down my ideas. "And what clues made you suspect these two?"

I smiled. "It's all a question of experience," I said.

I didn't mention my theory of about eyes. That's my little secret.

They don't call me Supersleuth for nothing.

About the Author

Barbara Mitchelhill started writing when she was seven years old. She says, "When I was eight or nine, I used to pretend I was a detective, just like Damian. My friend, Liz, and I used to watch people walking down our street and we would write clues in our notebooks. I don't remember catching any criminals!" She has written many books for children. She lives in Shropshire, England, and gets some of her story ideas when she walks her dogs, Jeff and Ella.

About the Illustrator

Tony Ross was born in London in 1938. He has illustrated lots of books, including some by Paula Danziger, Michael Palin, and Roald Dahl. He also writes and illustrates his own books. He has worked as a cartoonist, graphic designer, and art director of an advertising agency. When he was a kid, he wanted to grow up to be a cowboy.

Glossary

depressed (di-PREST)—sad

detective (di-TEK-tiv)—someone whose work is getting information about crimes and trying to solve them

forger (FORJ-ur)—someone who makes illegal copies of things, such as CDs, DVDs, or paintings

mission (MISH-un)—goal

scan (SKAN)—to look at quickly

sleuth (SLOOTH)—a detective

suspicious (suh-SPISH-uhss)—to think or feel that something may be wrong

swindlers (SWIND-lurz)—cheaters

technician (tek-NISH-uhn)—an expert in a specific skill or process

tutor (TOO-tur)—someone who teaches a student privately

Discussion Questions

1. What do you think of Damian's approach to solving crimes? What works? What does not work? Explain your answers.

2. Does Damian remind you of any other detectives you've read about or seen on television or in the movies? How does he compare? Explain.

3. On page 22, the director tells Damian to watch out for crooks. Does he really mean this? How do you know?

4. On page 49, when Damian gets in the car, do you consider him to be smart? Brave? Or is he not so brave or smart? Explain your answer and include what you would have done in that situation.

Writing Prompts

1. Write about why Damian leaves the scene of the crime (page 9). Why do you think he does not want publicity?

2. Damian says that "a real detective looks for clues." Write about what he means by this and how he gathers and uses his clues.

3. If you were a sleuth, would you wear a special disguise like Damian does? Would you have special business cards? How would you solve crimes? Write a story where you are the detective in a mystery, and describe what you would do to solve the case.

Read other adventures of Damian Drooth, Supersleuth

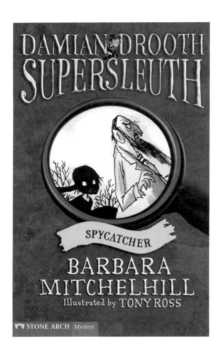

Spycatcher

There are spies in the neighborhood. Mr. Swan asks Damian Drooth to find out who is stealing his secret plans. Everyone has a part of the puzzle, but only Damian can fit them all together!

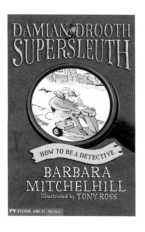

How to Be a Detective

Damian Drooth, Supersleuth, shares his stellar detective skills with the kids from school. When he leads the amateur detectives to the local dog show, things really start to get hairy!

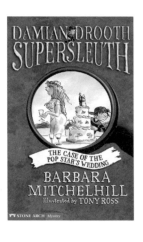

The Case of the Pop Star's Wedding

Damian puts his detective skills to the test when he is asked to guard the gifts at a famous pop star's wedding. Damian outwits a jewel thief, but is not so lucky with the giant wedding cake!

Internet Sites

Do you want to know more about subjects related to this book? Or are you interested in learning about other topics? Then check out FactHound, a fun, easy way to find Internet sites.

Our investigative staff has already sniffed out great sites for you!

Here's how to use FactHound:

1. Visit *www.facthound.com*

2. Select your grade level.

3. To learn more about subjects related to this book, type in the book's ISBN number: **1598891197**.

4. Click the **Fetch It** button.

FactHound will fetch the best Internet sites for you!